Published By TMC Books LLC

ISBN: 978-0-9826539-3-7

Library of Congress Control Number: 2011939072

Printed in Canada

I'd like to dedicate this book to my loving father Fremont, who has been known to be a bear in a restaurant.

TMC BOOKS LLC
731 Tasker Hill Rd,
Conway, NH 03818
USA
www.tmcbooks.com

Bears love to eat all kinds of things, when they're in the mood. They can walk right into restaurants, and enjoy some fancy food.

It's usually a shock to the patrons dining there.
People are not used to the idea of dining with a bear.

So they exit in a hurry, abandoning all their dishes.
What more could a bear want? It answers all their wishes.

The finest meals, both hot and cold, are there for you to take.

Foods, fried and steamed, sautéed and baked, and even lots of cake.

At just about all restaurants of every different kind, you see the same effect on diners; it happens every time.

The thought that bears can eat their food seems to move folks from their places. You can tell they're not quite pleased with this, by the looks upon their faces.

Enjoy yourself a plate or two, and grab yourself a snack.

Exit through the kitchen—I'm sure that when you're there, you'll find all kinds of yummy things, just suited for a bear.

School cafeterias also work just fine, if restaurants aren't around. The kiddies are afraid of bears, so they just won't be found.

You'll have some time to dine on pizza, pickles, mac and cheese...
Make sure you exit through the kitchen, trust me on this, please.

Parks are a place to snag a meal, when you're looking cute.
Folks who like to eat at parks, love to share their loot.

They want you to take the food from them, while they snap a picture.

Mosty they leave you sandwiches, but there could be quite a mixture. Chips and cookies, fruits and drinks, you don't even have to ask it. They'll up and run away from you, and leave you with a basket.

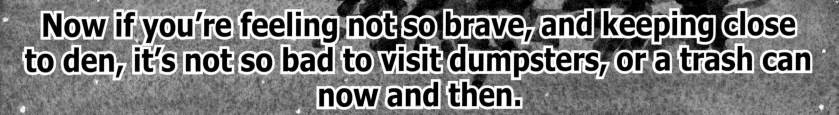

Now if you're feeling not so brave, and keeping close to den, it's not so bad to visit dumpsters, or a trash can now and then.

And there's always the berry patch, or beechnuts in the woods,

But if there's one tip I can leave you with—it's (trust me) o[ut of] the kitchen.

If you have to be a bear, you might as well have some fun.

Things to bring along while dining out:
Flashlight with extra batteries
Dental floss
Necktie
Handy wipes
Fly swatter
Appetite